Vendetta Fury

A Haunting Finale o a Criminal Family

Sarvagya Chugh

ISBN 978-93-5667-966-5
© Sarvagya Chugh 2023

Published in India 2023 by Pencil

A brand of
One Point Six Technologies Pvt. Ltd.
Unit no. 26, Ground Floor, Building A1,
Wadala Truck Terminal Road,
Near Post Office, Antop Hill, Mumbai - 400037
E connect@thepencilapp.com
W www.thepencilapp.com

Author biography

Sarvagya Chugh is a talented and aspiring author hailing from India. With a passion for writing that knows no bounds, he has embarked on a journey to captivate readers with his unique storytelling. At just 18 years old, Sarvagya showcases a remarkable depth of creativity and a remarkable ability to craft compelling narratives. "Vendetta Fury" marks his debut novel, leaving an indelible mark on the literary world. With his imaginative writing style and a promising future ahead, Sarvagya Chugh is a name to watch out for in the world of literature.

CONTENTS

Epigraph

Epigraph: "Revenge is a dish best served with fury, Where bloodlines entwine in a tragic story. In shadows and secrets, the truth shall rise, As brothers clash, in a deadly guise."

Sarvagya Chugh

Preface

In the depths of darkness, where vendettas brew and bloodlines intertwine, lies a tale of betrayal, vengeance, and shattered brotherhood. "Vendetta Fury" takes you on a relentless journey into a world where loyalty is tested, secrets unravel, and the line between justice and revenge blurs.

Within these pages, you will meet Affonso, a man torn between love and duty, and Kerrim, his own flesh and blood, consumed by an insatiable thirst for retribution. As their paths converge, a web of deceit is spun, leading to a climactic showdown where the ultimate price must be paid.

Through the vivid tapestry of characters and the atmospheric setting, this story explores the complexities of human nature, the bonds that tie us, and the choices that shape our destinies. Brace yourself for a gripping narrative filled with unexpected twists, heart-wrenching emotions, and moral dilemmas that will leave you questioning the very nature of justice.

So, venture forth, dear reader, and immerse yourself in the world of "Vendetta Fury," where the line between darkness and light fades, and the consequences of our actions resonate long after the final page is turned.

Acknowledgements

I would like to express my deepest gratitude to all those who have supported me on this incredible journey of writing "Vendetta Fury."

First and foremost, I extend my heartfelt appreciation to my family for their unwavering love, encouragement, and belief in my creative endeavors. Your constant support has been the driving force behind my aspirations.

I am indebted to my friends and beta readers who provided valuable feedback and constructive criticism, helping me refine the story and characters. Your insights and perspectives have truly enriched the narrative.

I am grateful to the literary community, fellow authors, and writing groups who have offered guidance, inspiration, and camaraderie along this writing journey. Your passion for storytelling continues to inspire me.

Lastly, I would like to express my deepest appreciation to the readers who embark on this adventure with me. Your enthusiasm and support for the written word make this all worthwhile.

To each and every one of you, thank you for being a part of "Vendetta Fury." This book would not have been possible without your contributions and belief in my abilities.

With heartfelt gratitude,

Sarvagya Chugh

Shadows of the Past

The dimly lit bar exuded an air of secrecy, with the soft murmurs of conversation mingling with the clinking of glasses. **Affonso Bellini**, a man of captivating presence and authority, sat across from his trusted confidant, **Antonino Mele**. Their eyes locked, a silent understanding passing between them as they delved into the depths of their family's empire and the profound loyalty that bound them.

Lodovico Rizzo, the third pillar of the sinister family enters the room with an impactful presence, the air heavy with anticipation. Their eyes met, conveying a shared understanding of the challenges that lay ahead.

Bellini sighed deeply; his voice laced with determination. "Lodovico, my brother, the world is changing. Our family's legacy hangs in the balance, and we must adapt to survive." Lodovico, his expression marked by a mix of concern and resolve, nodded in agreement. "Indeed, Bellini. The old ways are fading, and a new breed of criminals rises. We must be more careful than ever and resourceful."

Bellini leaned forward; his voice low but filled with conviction. "Our strength lies in unity, Lodovico. We have always been a family bound by loyalty and blood.

Together, we will face the challenges that come our way."

Lodovico's gaze held Bellini's, their unspoken bond carrying the weight of years spent side by side. "Bellini, we have overcome countless obstacles in the past. We have always stood together, and we shall continue to do so. Our enemies may change, but our resolve remains unshaken."

A flicker of determination ignited in Bellini's eyes. "You speak true, Lodovico. Our path forward will be treacherous, but we shall forge ahead with unwavering courage. We will adapt, evolve, and ensure our family's survival."

Lodovico nodded, a hint of a smile playing at the corners of his lips. "Together, we are invincible. We will face every challenge head-on and emerge stronger. Our legacy will endure, a testament to the Bellini name."

As they sat in the study, surrounded by the echoes of their ancestors, Bellini and Lodovico shared a moment of silent resolve. The path ahead was uncertain, but with their unwavering bond and the strength of their family, they knew they could face any storm that awaited them.

Raising his glass, Affonso smiled with a touch of mischief. "To the unbreakable loyalty that binds us, to the empire we've built with our blood, sweat, and tears "Together, we'll overcome any obstacle and crush any traitor who dares cross our path."

Antonino, and Lodovico lifted their glasses in unison, a shared determination shining in their eyes. "To the empire," they, their voices resonating with a mixture of unity and defiance.

Loyalties and Love

Within the opulent walls of the grand estate, bathed in the soft glow of candlelight, Affonso Bellini and **Nadya**, a captivating Russian beauty, found solace in each other's arms. Their love, a refuge from the treacherous world they inhabited, blossomed amidst the shadows of their shared secrets and desires.

The room resonated with the tender notes of a pianist, his fingers dancing across the keys, weaving a melody that mirrored the delicate emotions between Affonso and Nadya. The air was heavy with anticipation as they basked in the warmth of their connection, their laughter filling the space and mingling with the intoxicating scent of passion.

Affonso, his gaze fixed upon Nadya's radiant smile, spoke with a voice that held both strength and vulnerability. "Nadya, my love, in this directionless world, you are the anchor that steadies me. With you by my side, I find the courage to stand against the darkest depths of our reality."

Nadya's eyes shimmered with adoration as her fingers traced the contours of Affonso's face. "Affonso, my steadfast protector, our love is a beacon that illuminates the shadows. In your embrace, I discover solace amidst the chaos, a sanctuary of understanding."

Yet, unbeknownst to them, beneath the surface of their idyllic world, malevolent forces lurked, seeking to exploit their vulnerability and tear their empire apart.

Antonino Mele, Affonso's trusted agent and confidant, stood alongside him, his gaze focused on the labyrinthine web of alliances and betrayals that defined their existence. **Heinz Knopf**, the strategic mastermind behind their operations, observed the scene with a penetrating intensity, his mind forever analysing the chessboard of power.

"Antonino," Heinz began, his voice laced with caution, "we must tread carefully in these treacherous waters. The currents of betrayal run deep, threatening to undermine everything we have built.
 We must fortify our defences and remain vigilant against those who would seek to exploit our loyalty and threat this family."

Antonino nodded; his features etched with determination. "You speak the truth, Heinz. Trust has been the bedrock of our success, but it is a fragile foundation. We must be cautious, even with those closest to us, for the allure of power can turn even the most resolute souls. Our family's survival lies on our ability to protect it."

As the night wore on, the Specter of danger loomed ever larger. Unbeknownst to Affonso and his trusted allies, Kerrim, an enigmatic figure skilled in the art of manipulation, observed from the shadows.

A wolf in sheep's clothing, Kerrim harboured dark intentions, ready to sow the seeds of betrayal that would fracture the foundation of their empire.

The stage was set for a deadly dance, where love and loyalty would clash with deceit and ambition. The flames of passion burned bright, their warmth intertwined with the icy touch of treachery, as the destinies of these interconnected lives hurtled towards a fateful collision.

In the depths of their love, Affonso and Nadya found solace and strength, unaware of the storm that brewed on the horizon. The darkness would test their loyalties, pushing them to the brink of despair, as the enigmatic Kerrim executed a plan that would forever alter the course of their lives.

As the night waned and the echoes of their laughter faded, Affonso and Nadya clung to each other, their love a shield against the impending tempest. In the shadows, Kerrim's machinations gained momentum, his every move a step closer to the destruction that awaited them all.

The tapestry of their lives was intricately woven with love, loyalty, and treachery, bound to unravel in the most devastating of ways. The road ahead would be paved with bloodshed and heartache, challenging their resolve and testing the limits of their humanity.

Little did they know, as they embraced under the flickering candlelight, that the forces of darkness were converging upon them, threatening to dismantle their empire and leave them at the mercy of their own shattered loyalties.

Meanwhile on the other hand, As the days turned into weeks, the Bellini family began meticulously planning their next move—the heist that would secure their position and ensure their continued dominance, The Heist to uplift their confidence and knock down any questions arising for their sharpness, Bellini knew that this operation required careful coordination and a team of skilled individuals. He called upon Heinz, a master strategist, and a trusted ally, to assemble the crew.

Heinz, a man of few words but immense, wasted no time in gathering a team of experts in their respective fields. Each member possessed a unique set of skills that would be crucial to the success of the operation. They had spent weeks observing the warehouse, noting the patterns of guards, studying the security measures, and identifying potential vulnerabilities.

In a dimly lit room, the team gathered around a large table, spread with blueprints and surveillance photos of the warehouse. The atmosphere was charged with anticipation as the members shared their insights and devised a plan that would leave no room for error.

Heinz took charge, his voice filled with authority. "This heist will require precision, timing, and impeccable teamwork. We must be prepared for any unforeseen circumstances and have contingencies in place. Our objective is to secure the weapons and oil from the government's treasury and deliver a crippling blow to their operations."

One by one, the members of the team shared their ideas, discussing potential strategies and analysing the risks involved. The room buzzed with excitement and determination as each person contributed their expertise to the collective plan.

Bellini, observing the discussions with a keen eye, interjected, "Remember, our success depends on our ability to remain undercover. We cannot afford any slip-ups or compromises. Our priority is to retrieve the assets and leave without leaving a trace." He further added, "Our family will rise tomorrow to the highs along with the sun, and by the night, the government will be set to dawn alongside the sun"

The planning sessions stretched late into the night, the air thick with the weight of responsibility and the knowledge that failure was not an option. They refined their strategies, ironed out the details, and set strict timelines for each phase of the operation.

Weeks passed as the team continued to observe the warehouse, meticulously fine-tuning their plan. They familiarized themselves with every nook and cranny, every guard rotation, and every security measure. They were like shadows, unseen and unheard, silently waiting for the opportune moment to strike.

Throughout this period, tension grew within the team. The stakes were high, and the weight of the mission bore heavily on their shoulders. Doubts and insecurities crept into their minds, but the unbreakable bond of family and shared purpose kept them united.

In the depths of the night, as the moon cast an ethereal glow over their clandestine meeting place, Bellini addressed the team one final time before the heist. "This operation will test us in ways we've never experienced before. But I have complete faith in each and every one of you. We've trained for this, we've planned meticulously, and now it's time to execute."
With grim determination etched on their faces, the team dispersed, their minds filled with visions of success and the weight of responsibility that came with it.

They knew that their actions would reverberate throughout the underworld and determine the fate of the Bellini family.
The stage was set, the plans were laid, and the countdown began. In the silence of the night, the anticipation grew. The heist awaited, a daring feat that would test their skills, their loyalty, and their resilience.

To be continued...

Shadows of Deception

It was a Fine evening when,
Lodovico stood before Bellini, his face etched with a mixture of concern and compassion. In the dimly lit room, he mustered the courage to express his reservations.
"Bellini," Lodovico began, his voice filled with genuine concern, "I understand your drive for power and influence, but at what cost? The government's resources are meant to protect and serve the people, we will steal those resources for what better? Shouldn't we focus on improving our community instead of opposing them?"

Bellini met Lodovico's gaze, his eyes reflecting a deep determination and a touch of sadness. "Lodovico, my brother, I appreciate your kind heart and your noble intentions. But you must understand that the government's resources are not always employed for the greater good.

They are wielded like guns and oil, tools that can be used to destroy us, to suppress our freedom, and undermine our way of life."

He paced the room, his voice resonating with a sense of urgency. "We cannot simply wait for them to strike first. We must take the initiative and dismantle their power, for only then can we ensure the safety and prosperity of our family and our community."

Lodovico's brow furrowed as he struggled to reconcile his innate sense of compassion with Bellini's unyielding resolve. "But Bellini, what if there is another way? What if we can find a path that allows us to protect our family without resorting to violence and destruction?"

Bellini's expression hardened; his voice tinged with a touch of disappointment. "Lodovico, my brother, I admire your unwavering compassion. But the world we live in is one of darkness and treachery. It is a world where the power-hungry will stop at nothing to bring us down. We must be prepared to face the storm head-on and emerge victorious."

He drew closer to Lodovico, his eyes burning with determination. "We have been given the unique ability to shape our own destiny, to protect those we hold dear.
The heist we embark upon is not just an act of self-preservation but a statement of defiance against a system that seeks to oppress us. We must stand strong and show the world that we will not be subdued."

Lodovico sighed, his conflicted emotions palpable. "Bellini, I want to believe in your vision, but my heart is burdened by the potential consequences. Can we truly justify the destruction and violence that may result from our actions?"

Bellini placed a hand on Lodovico's shoulder, his voice filled with compassion. "Lodovico, my brother, I feel the weight of your uncertainty. But we are at a point, where our choices will shape the future. We cannot let fear and doubt hold us back from achieving greatness. Sometimes, sacrifices must be made for the greater good, even if they weigh heavily on our hearts."

Their eyes locked, and a profound silence enveloped the room. In that moment, the brothers understood each other's perspectives, the clash of idealism and pragmatism. They shared a bond forged through blood and loyalty, even in the face of uncertainty.

"Lodovico," Bellini said, his voice softening, "I know this path is fraught with risks and sacrifices. But we must remain steadfast in our resolve. Together, we can navigate the treacherous waters ahead, and emerge stronger than ever before. Our family's legacy depends on it."

Lodovico nodded slowly, his eyes reflecting a mixture of hesitation and trust. "I will stand by your side, Bellini. But let us remember the value of compassion and mercy, even in the darkest of times. We must find a way to protect our family without losing our humanity."

Bellini's lips curled into a slight smile. "Agreed, my brother. We shall strive to be not just powerful, but also compassionate leaders. Our actions will speak volumes, and we shall forge a path that balances strength with empathy."

Their hearts are heavy with the weight of their impending mission, Lodovico and Bellini embraced, their bond reaffirmed. They knew that the journey ahead would be filled with challenges, but together, they would face them head-on.

As they stepped into the unknown, their destinies intertwined, the echoes of their conversation lingered in the air, a testament to the complex duality of their aspirations and the power of brotherhood.

It was an era when the clutches of industrialization began to tighten their grip on society, yet the art of thievery remained a dark and mysterious craft. The team of five, a band of seasoned criminals and masters of their trade, embarked on a mission that would test their skills and loyalty to the core.
Their target: the heavily fortified treasury of the government, where weapons and oil reserves were stored. It was a daring endeavour, one that would not only cripple the government's resources but also serve as a symbol of their defiance against the powers that sought to control them.

Under the cover of a moonless night, the team assembled on the outskirts of the city, their faces obscured by shadow and determination etched upon their features. Affonso Bellini, the charismatic leader, surveyed his companions, his voice low and commanding.

" We will undertake a heist that will shake the very foundation of power, shock the realm" Affonso declared, his words carrying the weight of their audacious plan. "Within those walls lies not only the means to arm their forces but also the lifeblood of their empire. We will take their strength, leaving them vulnerable and exposed."

The team nodded in unison; their resolve unwavering. They had trained tirelessly, each member bringing their unique set of skills to the table. Antonino Mele, the agile and nimble infiltrator, possessed a gift for unlocking even the most intricate of locks. Heinz Knopf, the strategic mastermind, orchestrated the operation with calculated precision. Lodovico Rizzo, the experienced crime master, brought an air of ruthlessness and resourcefulness. And the other two members, shrouded in mystery, were the silent but deadly assassins, their true identities known only to a select few.

They made their way through the labyrinthine streets, their footsteps muffled by the stillness of the night. Their journey led them to the outskirts of the treasury, an imposing fortress bathed in darkness. There were no modern sensors or surveillance cameras to thwart their progress, but the ancient security measures were no less formidable.

The team approached the treasury with caution, aware that one wrong move could trigger an alarm, summoning an army of guards. Antonino, their master infiltrator, surveyed the surroundings, his keen eyes scanning for any signs of danger. With calculated precision, he disabled the locks and silently slipped through the entrance, motioning for his comrades to follow.

Inside, they encountered a labyrinth of corridors, guarded by patrolling sentinels. The team moved with a careful blend of stealth and speed, slipping past unsuspecting guards and avoiding detection. Each member played their part flawlessly, their movements synchronized as if choreographed.

But the path to the vault was not without its challenges. They encountered ancient booby traps, intricate mechanisms designed to protect the treasury's valuable contents.

With expert finesse, they bypassed pressure plates and avoided tripwires, relying on their knowledge of traditional trap-making techniques.

As they neared their objective, a sense of anticipation hung in the air. The vault door stood as an impenetrable barrier, its ancient construction a testament to the secrets it safeguarded.

It was here that Lodovico, the crime master, stepped forward, his eyes gleaming with determination.

With a combination of intuition and experience, Lodovico deciphered the intricate puzzle lock, the gears turning with a satisfying click. The massive vault door creaked open, revealing a treasure trove of weapons and barrels of oil.

Their hearts quickened with excitement as they moved swiftly, loading the stolen goods onto carts prepared for their escape. The weight of their mission settled upon their shoulders; the gravity of their actions was inescapable.

But as fate would have it, tragedy struck in the form of a bizarre accident. In a twist of cruel irony, Lodovico found himself caught in a perilous situation while attempting to save an innocent family caught in the crossfire. The sound of approaching police sirens shattered the stillness, and without hesitation, Lodovico made a split-second decision to divert the attention of the authorities, allowing his teammates a chance to escape.

The ensuing gunfight was fierce and relentless, reminiscent of a battle scene from a bygone era. The team fought with the fervor of survival, their pistols blazing, echoing through the vaulted halls. Dust and debris filled the air as bullets whizzed past, shattering ancient artifacts and stained-glass windows.

Each member displayed their unique skills, their training paying off as they skilfully maneuvered through the chaos. The echoes of gunshots and the cries of the wounded filled the air, mingling with the scent of gunpowder.

Despite their prowess, the odds were against them. They were outnumbered and outgunned by the relentless forces of law and order.

Affonso's heart raced with desperation and anguish as he approached Lodovico, their eyes locking in a moment of shared understanding.

Affonso: "Lodovico, we must go. The police are closing in, and we cannot afford to be captured."

Lodovico's eyes flickered with defiance, his resolve unyielding.

Lodovico: "I cannot abandon those innocent lives we swore to protect, Affonso. I will not leave them to the mercy of the law."

Affonso's voice cracked with emotion as he pleaded with his brother.

Affonso: "Lodovico, I understand your noble intentions, but we have a duty to our family. If you stay, you risk not only your own freedom but the very essence of who we are."
Lodovico's gaze softened, his voice tinged with resignation.

Lodovico: "Affonso, I cannot turn my back on those in need. It is who I am, and it is what our family stands for."
Tears welled up in Affonso's eyes as he grasped Lodovico's shoulders, his voice filled with a mixture of love and despair.

Affonso: "You are the embodiment of selflessness, Lodovico, a beacon of compassion in this dark world. But we cannot lose sight of what is at stake. Our family needs us."

Lodovico's eyes glistened with unshed tears as he nodded, the weight of his decision evident in his trembling voice.
Lodovico: "Affonso, promise me that you will protect our family, that you will carry on our mission, even if it means leaving me behind."

Affonso's voice cracked with emotion as he made a solemn vow.
Affonso: "I swear it, Lodovico. I will protect our family, and I will honour your sacrifice. Your bravery will not be forgotten."

They shared a final embrace, the weight of their unspoken words lingering in the air. With a heavy heart, Affonso turned away, his footsteps heavy with the burden of leaving his beloved brother behind.

Lodovico watched as Affonso disappeared into the shadows, his heart torn between the duty to his family and the calling of his conscience. As the sound of approaching police grew louder, he steeled himself for what lay ahead, knowing that his sacrifice would not be in vain.

In that moment, they both knew that this sacrifice was not only about saving others but about preserving the essence of their family. It was a testament to their unwavering commitment to justice and loyalty, a bond that could not be broken, even in the face of adversity.

And so, with tear-filled eyes and a heavy heart, Affonso left Lodovico behind, hoping that one day they would be reunited, and their family would stand strong once more.
Lodovico, ever the protector, fought valiantly, but in the face of overwhelming opposition, he was captured. His selfless act of sacrifice resonated deeply within the hearts of his comrades, filling them with a mix of sorrow, anger, and determination.

As the remaining members of the team made their daring escape, their minds were clouded with conflicting emotions. The weight of Lodovico's absence hung heavy, his fate uncertain. They mourned the loss of a brother in arms, fearing that he was gone forever.
Their steps were heavy as they retreated into the night, carrying the stolen weapons and oil with them. They vowed to honour Lodovico's sacrifice, to complete the

mission in his memory, and to unravel the mysteries that lay ahead.

Little did they know that their journey had only just begun, and the shadows of deception would continue to haunt them in the chapters yet to come.

First Meeting

As the dust settled from their harrowing escape, Affonso and Antonino were determined to find allies who shared their vision of justice and loyalty. They embarked on a mission to seek out individuals who possessed the skills and determination necessary to stand beside them in their quest.

Their journey led them to a dimly lit underground establishment, a haven for those who operated in the shadows. Among the crowd of dubious characters, their gaze landed on a figure who exuded an air of mystery and confidence. It was Kerrim, a man whose reputation whispered through the corridors of the criminal underworld.

Curiosity piqued, Affonso approached Kerrim, his eyes shining with a mixture of intrigue and skepticism.

"Excuse me, are you Kerrim?"
Kerrim's piercing gaze met Affonso's, a glint of recognition in his eyes. "And who might you be?" he responded, his voice carrying an undertone of guarded curiosity.

"I am Affonso, and this is my brother Antonino. We've been searching for someone with your unique set of skills. We've heard stories of your prowess and the impact you've made in the underground world."

Antonino, his voice filled with a hint of scepticism, chimed in. "We need individuals who possess unwavering loyalty, someone who can stand beside us in our pursuit of justice. Are you that person?"

Kerrim's lips curled into a faint smile, a knowing glimmer in his eyes. "Justice, loyalty, and the pursuit of a higher purpose. These are values I hold dear. But how can I be sure that your cause is worthy?"

Affonso's voice resonated with conviction as he explained their family's unwavering commitment to justice and loyalty. The spoke of their struggles, their triumphs, and their unyielding determination to protect the innocent.

"We believe in the power of unity, in assembling a formidable force to combat the forces of corruption. Together, we can dismantle those who exploit the weak and bring balance to a world plagued by darkness."

Kerrim's gaze lingered on Affonso and Antonino, weighing their words with careful consideration. He nodded, a flicker of intrigue crossing his face. "Very well. I'll offer you the opportunity to prove your intentions. If your cause is genuine, I'll stand beside you."

Affonso extended his hand, sealing the unspoken agreement between them. "Welcome to our family, Kerrim. Together, we will leave an indelible mark on the world."

In the days that followed, Affonso and Antonino witnessed firsthand Kerrim's unmatched skills and unwavering dedication. Kerrim's audacity and ability to adapt to any situation left them in awe. He demonstrated an uncanny talent for gathering information, infiltrating rival organizations, and executing precise manoeuvres that seemed almost otherworldly.

As the three men engaged in intense training sessions, their bond grew stronger. Affonso and Antonino marvelled at Kerrim's exceptional abilities, recognizing that they had found a true ally in their quest for justice. They could see the potential of their united force, an unstoppable team ready to challenge the forces that threatened their family.

In a moment of reflection, Affonso turned to Kerrim, his eyes filled with gratitude. "Kerrim, you have surpassed our expectations. Your loyalty and commitment to our cause are commendable. Together, we will achieve great things."

Kerrim's voice resonated with determination as he replied, "I have found a purpose greater than myself in your family. Together, we will leave an indelible mark on the world, a testament to the power of loyalty and justice."

And so, united by a shared purpose, the trio embarked on a journey that would test their mettle and redefine their destinies. With Kerrim's unique skills and unwavering loyalty added to their ranks, they stood ready to face whatever challenges lay ahead, confident that their unity would lead them to victory.

His arrival brought a glimmer of hope to their fractured unity, a flickering light in the face of uncertainty. They saw in him the potential to restore balance and stability to their operations. The family, desperate for a sense of normalcy amidst the chaos, welcomed him with open arms, unaware of the darkness that lurked beneath his façade.

Kerrim, ever the master manipulator, skilfully guided conversations, subtly planting seeds of doubt and mistrust within the hearts of his unwitting targets. He saw in Antonino Mele, a loyal confidant of Affonso, an opportunity to sow the seeds of discord. With carefully chosen words, he began to insinuate that Affonso's affections for Nadya overshadowed his devotion to the family, casting doubt on their unity and threatening to erode their bonds.

However, Mele, a pillar of strength and loyalty, stood firm against Kerrim's insidious attempts to tarnish Affonso's character. He saw through the veil of manipulation, recognizing the true nature of their leader's love for Nadya. Mele's unwavering support and defines of Affonso became a testament to their brotherly bond, a declaration that their unity would not be shattered by baseless accusations.

As the chapter unfolded, the cracks in trust deepened, but the family remained oblivious to Kerrim's true motives. His guidance of their conversations seemed innocuous, his presence a reassuring presence. Yet, beneath the surface, his web of deception expanded, threatening to ensnare them all in a trap of his making.

Only time would reveal Kerrim's true intentions and the extent of his manipulative prowess. The family, blissfully unaware of the storm that brewed within their midst, continued their struggle with internal conflicts and the looming threat to Lodovico's life. Their fate teetered on a precipice, and the web of deceit spun by Kerrim tightened its grip, inch by insidious inch.

Kerrim caught Antonino in a casual conversation while polishing guns, Kerrim smiled, a smile that held both malice and intrigue. "Ah, Antonino, you are a loyal friend indeed. But are you not blinded by your own devotion? Open your eyes and see the truth that lies beneath the surface. Affonso's actions speak louder than words. He left Lodovico behind in Rome without so much as a second thought. Can a true brother do such a thing?"

Mele's brow furrowed, his mind grappling with the accusation. Doubt seeped into the corners of his thoughts, like a persistent shadow threatening to engulf him. But he refused to let it take hold. "No, Kerrim. Affonso's love for Nadya does not make him heartless. There must be reasons beyond our comprehension for his choices. I will not forsake my faith in him."

As the days turned into weeks, tensions simmered within the family. The weight of Lodovico's fate bore heavily upon their collective consciousness. Each member found themselves questioning the motives and actions of their loved ones.

The harmony that had once defined them was replaced by an undercurrent of suspicion and mistrust.

In the midst of this turmoil, Affonso struggled to reconcile his love for Nadya with his sense of duty. His heart pulled him in one direction, while his loyalty to the family demanded another. The internal battles waged within him, tearing at the very fabric of his being.

Meanwhile, news of the ongoing investigation in Rome reached their ears. The possibility of Lodovico being coerced into turning against his own family loomed over them like a Specter of doom. Affonso, knowing that their control in Rome was limited, made the difficult decision to wait, to bide their time until they could ascertain the true extent of the danger.

The weight of responsibility settled upon Affonso's shoulders, his mind consumed with the fate of Lodovico and the survival of the family. He knew that rushing into action without proper information could jeopardize everything they had built. Patience became their greatest ally, even as doubt and uncertainty threatened to tear them apart.

And in the shadows, Kerrim watched, his manipulative machinations edging them closer to the precipice of self-destruction. He remained the puppeteer, orchestrating their doubts and insecurities with precision. His presence went unnoticed, as the family directed their suspicions elsewhere, blinded by their own internal conflicts.

As Chapter 4 came to a close, the crack in their trust widened, and the darkness within their midst grew deeper. The fate of Lodovico remained uncertain, and the delicate balance they had maintained teetered on the edge. The road ahead was shrouded in shadows, and the family's destiny hung in the balance.

Little did they know that the true danger lay not in the external threats they faced, but in the fractures that threatened to tear them apart from within. Their unity, their very existence, depended on their ability to confront their doubts, to rise above the whispers of manipulation, and to rediscover the unbreakable bonds that had once defined them.

Rising Tension

The air crackled with tension as Affonso Bellini, the head of the family, sat at the head of a long mahogany table in the dimly lit room. His eyes burned with a mixture of anger and determination, fuelled by the recent attacks from the rival gang, **Veneto Nostra**, led by the ruthless **Gastone Buccino.**The loss of Lodovico Rizzo, their trusted crime master, still hung heavy in their hearts, and Bellini knew they needed to strike back with a vengeance.

Around the table, his loyal compatriots, including Antonino Mele and the enigmatic Kerrim, awaited his command.

The room reverberated with hushed whispers and uneasy glances, the absence of Lodovico creating a void that could not be filled. But Bellini was resolute. They had faced challenges before, and this would be no different.

"Listen, my brothers," Bellini began, his voice resonating with authority. "Veneto Nostra seeks to undermine our empire, to strike fear into the hearts of our people, advantaging Lodovico's absence. But we will not cower. We will show them the true strength of our family, the relentless force that lies within us."

His gaze locked with each member of his trusted circle, instilling a sense of purpose and unwavering loyalty. Kerrim, his eyes gleaming with determination, knew that this was his moment to prove his worth, to solidify his place among them.

"Kerrim," Bellini continued, his voice measured yet filled with intensity, "you have shown great skill and resourcefulness since joining our ranks. You will be instrumental in this mission. We need to strike a blow that will leave Veneto Nostra reeling, to remind them that we are not to be trifled with."

Kerrim nodded, a silent vow etched upon his features. He knew the weight of the task that lay before him, the responsibility of eradicating the threat that loomed over their family. He had studied the tactics and strategies of Veneto Nostra meticulously, searching for weaknesses to exploit.

As the meeting progressed, the plan for Mission Sanguigno Bellum took shape. It would be an audacious operation, designed to cripple Veneto Nostra and restore their family's dominance. The objective was clear – to strike at the heart of their rival's operations, dismantling their network and seizing control of their territories.

The mission would require stealth, precision, and fierce resolve. Kerrim outlined the intricate details, highlighting the vulnerable spots where they could exploit the rival gang's defences. He spoke with conviction, his words resonating with a quiet confidence that began to quell the doubts lingering within the room.

While Bellini and Mele were still grappling with the absence of Lodovico, Kerrim had seamlessly integrated himself into their ranks, his dedication and skill earning the respect of the family. But as Nadya, Bellini's beloved, observed the exchange from a distance, a flicker of suspicion danced in her eyes. She sensed something beneath Kerrim's composed facade, a hidden agenda that could unravel everything they had fought for.

Nadya's instincts compelled her to probe deeper, to uncover the truth behind Kerrim's motivations. She had seen the way he had maneuvered through conversations, subtly guiding their thoughts and redirecting their focus.

While Bellini and Mele remained entranced by Kerrim's charm, Nadya remained vigilant, determined to protect the family from any hidden threats.

As the meeting concluded, the room buzzed with a newfound sense of purpose. Bellini, Mele, and Kerrim shared a solemn nod, their determination etched upon their faces. They would execute Mission Sanguigno Bellum flawlessly, exacting their revenge upon Veneto Nostra and securing their family's position in the criminal underworld.

Days turned into nights as they meticulously prepared for the operation. Each member honed their skills, fine-tuning their instincts to act as one cohesive unit. The gravity of the situation weighed heavily upon them, the realization that this would be their first major endeavor without the guiding hand of Lodovico Rizzo.

Meanwhile, news reached their ears of an internal investigation involving Lodovico in Rome. The threat of his betrayal loomed, a dark cloud casting doubt upon their already fragile state of affairs. Bellini resisted the urge to act rashly, knowing that they held little control over events unfolding in distant corners of the city. Instead, he focused his energies on the mission at hand.

Tensions ran high within the Bellini household. The weight of their past losses and the impending battle threatened to fracture their unity. But as they gathered around the dinner table, a sense of camaraderie and determination began to mend the cracks in their foundation.

Unknown to them, Kerrim had received information regarding a traitor within their midst. One of their own had leaked the family's strategy papers and blueprints to Veneto Nostra. Bellini's rage surged, demanding immediate retribution, but Kerrim intervened, his voice a calming presence amid the storm.

"Patience, Bellini," Kerrim whispered, his voice filled with an air of calculated control. "Let us handle this matter discreetly. We shall extract the truth from the traitor and ensure justice is served."

Bellini reluctantly relented, his anger simmering beneath the surface. Three days later, the agent returned, oblivious to the danger that awaited him. The family feigned ignorance, acting as if they were none the wiser.

Kerrim, wearing a mask of cordiality, commended the agent on his supposed loyalty, inviting him to share a celebratory dinner. The agent hesitated, sensing a shift in the atmosphere, but ultimately accepted the invitation.

As the night wore on, the atmosphere grew increasingly tense. Kerrim skilfully steered the conversation, delving into the agent's loyalties and involvement with Veneto Nostra. In a moment of vulnerability, the agent revealed the depths of his treachery, unknowingly sealing his fate.

With a swift, calculated move, Kerrim tightened the ropes that bound the agent, exposing the truth to Bellini and Nadya. The room fell silent as the weight of betrayal hung in the air.

"This is the price of disloyalty," Kerrim declared, his voice laced with an icy determination. "Our family is built on trust, and those who dare to betray us shall meet their deserved fate."

With a chilling resolve, Kerrim led the bound agent to Bellini's private quarters, where Nadya and Bellini awaited. The agent's eyes widened with fear, realizing the gravity of his actions. In a shocking display of loyalty and ruthlessness, Kerrim fired 23 bullets into the agent's body, extinguishing the treacherous flame that threatened to consume them all.

As the room was bathed in silence, Bellini and Nadya exchanged a knowing glance. The events of that night had reaffirmed their faith in Kerrim and his unwavering dedication to their cause. They understood that to protect their family, sacrifices had to be made, and the line between right and wrong had blurred.

Mission Sanguigno Bellum loomed on the horizon, promising an epic clash between the Bellini family and Veneto Nostra. In the wake of the agent's demise, their resolve burned brighter, and their determination solidified.

 Kerrim had proven himself as an indispensable asset, their shield against external threats and internal disloyalty.

However, Nadya's suspicions persisted, her intuition warning her of the complexity lurking beneath Kerrim's facade. As they ventured deeper into the treacherous world of organized crime, she vowed to uncover the truth, safeguarding her loved ones from any hidden dangers that may threaten their unity and the fragile balance of trust that held them together.

Mission Sanguigno Bellum

The night was cloaked in darkness as the Bellini family prepared to execute their most audacious mission yet. Mission Sanguigno Bellum, a name whispered with equal parts fear and anticipation held the key to their dominance over their rival gang, Veneto Nostra. Kerrim, the enigmatic figure with a past shrouded in shadows, stood at the forefront of this operation, his cunning and ruthlessness their greatest asset.

The venue of the fateful encounter was a dilapidated warehouse, a fortress of secrecy for the rival gang. Kerrim, with his masterful manipulation and knowledge of the agent who had leaked crucial information, assumed a false identity. He presented himself as the agent's long-lost brother, weaving a web of deception that would ensnare the rival gang leader, Gastone Buccio.

With a mischievous glint in his eyes, Kerrim approached Buccio, his voice filled with a mixture of sorrow and anger. He revealed intimate details of the agent's life, divulging information that only Buccio could have known. The rival gang leader's curiosity was piqued, and his guard momentarily lowered.

"He died for you," Kerrim whispered, his voice laced with a subtle menace. "Now, I have come to claim what is rightfully ours."

Intrigued by the prospect of new information and seeking solace in his grief, Buccio followed Kerrim to a secluded room. The air crackled with tension as Kerrim executed a masterstroke of betrayal. With swift precision, he silenced Buccio, preventing any outcry that could alert the gang members outside, and stabbed him with a sharp knife.

Kerrim told Buccio "If you want to play in the Elite league, then be elite, you Fu****g A**, don't try to play with an amateur gang, now go to the forever sleep, that is provided to you by a master of crimes, Good Night Buccio"

Meanwhile, the rest of the Bellini family and their loyal agents, armed to the teeth, stood ready for the onslaught. Bellini, Mele, and the team of five, their hearts pounding with anticipation, awaited the signal to storm the warehouse. Kerrim's role was pivotal—their success hinged on his ability to eliminate Buccio and open the gates for their entrance.

As Kerrim emerged from the room, his demeanour composed and his face a mask of concern, he calmly informed the waiting agents that Buccio had suffered a sudden heart attack. Urgency gripped the gang members as they rushed to their leader's aid, their guard momentarily relaxed.

In that fleeting moment, Kerrim seized the opportunity. He discreetly opened the door, signalling to his fellow agents that the path was clear. With steely resolve, they infiltrated the warehouse, bullets whizzing through the air as the battle erupted in a symphony of chaos and violence.

The clash was fierce, the echoes of gunfire reverberating through the cavernous space. The Bellini family fought with unwavering determination; their resolve unyielding. The odds seemed insurmountable, but their unity and skill proved formidable.

However, as the battle raged on, the family found themselves outnumbered. Their resources stretched thin; they knew they had to make a strategic retreat. With Kerrim leading the way, they fought their way to an exit, leaving a trail of fallen enemies in their wake.

The Bellini family emerged from the warehouse, victorious yet weary. They had achieved their objective—the elimination of Buccio and his brother. The rival gang lay shattered, their leadership decimated. The balance of power had shifted, and the Bellini family stood as the reigning force in the criminal underworld.

As they regrouped in the aftermath of the mission, a mix of relief and exhaustion hung in the air. Kerrim, his mask of loyalty still firmly in place, surveyed his comrades. His role in their triumph remained hidden, his true intentions known only to himself.

But amidst the celebration, Nadya's suspicions lingered.

She observed Kerrim, his calculated actions and hidden agendas. Her intuition told her that there was more to him than met the eye.
Determined to uncover the truth, she resolved to keep a watchful eye on their enigmatic new ally.
Little did she know that Kerrim's past, steeped in bloodshed and ambition, held secrets that could shake the very foundation of the Bellini family. And as their trust in each other wavered, the stakes grew higher, setting the stage for a battle not only against external enemies but also the demons within.

As the echoes of the battle began to fade, the surviving members of the Bellini family gathered to take stock of their victory. Adrenaline coursed through their veins; their bodies weary but their spirits soaring. In the midst of the celebration, Kerrim stood at the centre of their admiration.

Bellini, Mele, and the rest of the family praised Kerrim for his cunning tactics and unwavering loyalty. They applauded his instrumental role in dismantling Veneto Nostra and securing their dominance. His skills and resourcefulness had proven invaluable, and their gratitude flowed freely.

However, amidst the joyous accolades, an unsettling rumour began to circulate. Whispers carried on the wind, hinting at a tragedy that struck a blow to the heart of the Bellini family. News had reached them, unconfirmed but with ominous weight, that Lodovico had met his end at the hands of the police.

The mere possibility of such a loss cast a sombre shadow over their celebrations. Lodovico, the charismatic leader, and beloved brother, was the pillar of their strength. The bond they shared, forged through years of loyalty and brotherhood, was unbreakable. The thought of his demise struck deep at their core, leaving them vulnerable and questioning their own mortality.

Amidst the lingering uncertainty, the family gathered in solemn silence, their thoughts consumed by the news that hung heavy in the air. They clung to hope, praying that the rumour would prove false, that Lodovico would emerge unscathed from the darkness that threatened to engulf them.

As the days passed, tension simmered beneath the surface, each member grappling with their own fears and doubts. Kerrim, though hailed as a hero, felt the weight of his newfound responsibility.

He recognized the significance of Lodovico's absence and the void it created within the family's dynamics. In the depths of his eyes, a flicker of remorse and guilt danced, hidden from prying gazes.

Nadya, torn between her love for Lodovico and her growing suspicions of Kerrim, found herself caught in a whirlwind of conflicting emotions. The uncertainty surrounding Lodovico's fate gnawed at her, fuelling her determination to uncover the truth behind Kerrim's enigmatic facade.

But as they navigated the treacherous waters of doubt and grief, the Bellini family remained resolute. They clung to the bond that united them, drawing strength from their shared purpose and unyielding determination.

 They vowed to honour Lodovico's memory, regardless of his fate, and to continue the legacy of the family he had built.

And so, in the face of uncertain times and mounting challenges, the Bellini family stood united. Together, they would confront the harsh realities that lay ahead, their trust in one another tested but unbroken. For they knew that in the world they inhabited, where loyalty was paramount and danger lurked at every turn, their strength lay in the bonds of blood and the unwavering resolve of their shared purpose.

The news of Lodovico's fate remained shrouded in uncertainty, a Specter that haunted their thoughts. Yet, they pressed on, fuelled by the memories of their fallen comrades and the burning desire to secure their place in the criminal underworld.

To be continued...

Sense Of Hope

The cloudy sky cast a sombre hue over the Bellini estate as the family gathered to finalize their plan of escape for Lodovico. Nadya, sensing the weight of the impending mission, sought solace in the presence of Affonso. They found themselves drawn to each other, seeking comfort and strength amidst the brewing storm.

As the two sat together, their voices carried whispers of concern and determination. Affonso's eyes reflected the tumultuous thoughts swirling within him, while Nadya's unwavering resolve mirrored her loyalty to the family. They discussed the intricacies of the plan, mapping out each step with meticulous detail.

Meanwhile, Kerrim took charge, assembling the team and assigning tasks. He knew that the success of their mission hinged on careful planning and the element of surprise. With Lodovico's life hanging in the balance, there was no room for error.

Under the dimly lit room, the air thick with anticipation, Kerrim unveiled his strategy. He outlined the traps and diversions that would be set along the route of the police convoy. Each member of the team listened intently, committing every detail to memory. They knew that their lives, and the life of their beloved leader, depended on their flawless execution.

The plan involved strategically placed roadblocks, false emergencies, and decoy vehicles. Kerrim's network, carefully cultivated over years of undercover work, provided them with valuable information about the police convoy's route. With this knowledge, they could anticipate the locations where traps would be most effective.

Kerrim's voice carried authority as he addressed the team, his words a symphony of determination and unity. "Tomorrow, we face our darkest hour," he declared, his gaze sweeping over the room, meeting the eyes of each family member. "But we are Bellinis, bound by loyalty and fortified by our unwavering bond. We will overcome every obstacle
and ensure the safe return of our leader."

The room fell silent, each member of the family grappling with a mix of fear and determination. Antonino, his eyes burning with a fire that had never wavered, stepped forward. "I am ready," he proclaimed, his voice steady and resolute. "I trust in the strength and skill of my family. Together, we will face whatever lies ahead."

The night wore on, the atmosphere electric with a blend of anxiety and anticipation. Bellini, his heart heavy with the weight of his darkest imaginings, struggled to maintain composure. He knew the risks they faced, the shadows that threatened to consume them all.

As the dawn approached, the weather mirrored the somber mood. The clouds loomed overhead, casting a pall over the land. The time had come to set their plan into motion, to confront the demons that lurked on their path.

With hearts pounding and adrenaline surging through their veins, the Bellini family prepared to execute their meticulously devised plan. Each member took their assigned position, ready to act in perfect synchrony.

Kerrim's presence provided a sense of calm amidst the storm, his leadership guiding them forward.

The rain poured relentlessly, each drop echoing Affonso's inner turmoil as he stood alone, his gaze fixed on the darkened sky. Lost in his thoughts, he was unaware of Kerrim's approach until the sound of footsteps cut through the steady rhythm of the rainfall.

Kerrim, his figure shrouded by the rain-soaked night, walked slowly towards Affonso. His voice carried a mix of concern and determination as he broke the silence. "What weighs heavy on your mind, my dear friend?" he asked, his tone laced with genuine curiosity.

Affonso turned to face Kerrim, his face etched with worry. "Lodovico's escape," he replied, his voice filled with a mix of anxiety and determination. "The thought of losing him, of failing to protect him, it haunts me."

Kerrim's gaze softened as he placed a reassuring hand on Affonso's shoulder. "We will find a way, my friend," he assured him, his voice steady and unwavering. "We have come so far, overcome countless challenges. We won't let our leader slip through our fingers."

Affonso's brows furrowed; his gaze intense. "Kerrim, you may not understand. My father, Lucas Bellini, never wanted me to be a part of this world. He urged me to choose a different path, away from the shadows that consumed our family. But I couldn't resist the allure, the intoxicating power that comes with being a Bellini."

Kerrim listened attentively, his eyes reflecting understanding. "We all have our reasons for choosing this life," he replied, his voice tinged with empathy. "But I sense the shadows, too, Affonso. A storm looms on the horizon, threatening to unravel all that we've built. It may strike in a day, a week, or a month, but its presence is undeniable."

Affonso's eyes widened, his heart pounding within his chest. "How do you know, Kerrim? What signs do you see?" he asked, his voice trembling with a mix of fear and anticipation.
Kerrim's expression turned grave, his gaze piercing through the rain-soaked night.

"I have spent my life navigating the treacherous waters of the underworld, Affonso," he replied, his voice a whisper carried by the wind. "My instincts, honed by years of survival, tell me that something sinister lurks in the shadows. We must remain vigilant, prepared for whatever may come."

Affonso nodded, his resolve hardening. "We stand as Bellinis, united in our purpose," he declared, his voice filled with determination. "No matter the darkness that looms, we will face it together. Our family's legacy is too important to be overshadowed by fear."

As the rain continued to fall, Affonso and Kerrim shared a moment of silent understanding. In the face of uncertainty, their bond grew stronger, their commitment to protect their family unyielding. The storm may be approaching, but with Kerrim's guidance and their unbreakable resolve, they would weather whatever challenges lay ahead.

The day held the promise of both salvation and tragedy. The traps were set, the diversions prepared. The convoy carrying Lodovico would soon be on its fateful journey, unaware of the storm that awaited them.

The Rescued Brotherhood

The morning sun bathed the landscape in a golden hue as the Bellini family prepared to execute their daring mission to rescue Lodovico. With tension and anticipation in the air, Kerrim, the mastermind behind the plan, meticulously positioned the team of five at the entry point of the secluded path. Each member of the team was a seasoned professional, handpicked for their skills and unwavering loyalty.

Antonino, Bellini's trusted right-hand man, stood by his side halfway through the route. His stern expression masked the anxiety that gnawed at his insides. He knew the risks involved but remained steadfast in his commitment to the family.

High atop the surrounding hills, three expert snipers lay concealed, their scopes trained on the approaching convoy. Their focus was unwavering, their fingers lightly resting on the triggers of their rifles. They were the guardians of the operation, ready to eliminate any threats that
dared to challenge the family's resolve.

The atmosphere was charged with nervous energy as Kerrim reviewed the plan one final time. Each member of the team understood their role and the gravity of the situation. The success of the mission hinged on their flawless execution and unwavering determination.

As the army jeeps approached, Kerrim's heart pounded in his chest. The tension was palpable as they neared the designated entry point. However, just as the plan was about to unfold, a surge of panic rippled through the group. The driver of the lead army van had spotted the spike trap laid by Kerrim and swiftly veered away, avoiding the danger that lay in wait.

The sudden change in direction threw Kerrim off balance, but his quick-thinking mind refused to succumb to defeat. In a matter of seconds, he recalibrated his strategy, signalling the snipers to take aim at the vans as they diverted from the planned route. Smoke grenades were hurled into the air, filling the surroundings with a thick, impenetrable cloud.

Within the chaos and confusion, Kerrim and his team of five moved swiftly and silently through the smoke, their training guiding their every step. The thick shroud provided them with cover, obscuring their movements from prying eyes. Their hearts pounded with adrenaline as they advanced towards their objective.

Meanwhile, Bellini and Antonino, positioned in their getaway vehicle, accelerated with precision. The engine roared to life as they ploughed into the escort vehicles, causing a cacophony of screeching metal and shattering glass. The sudden impact created the perfect diversion, drawing attention away from Kerrim's team.

In the midst of the chaotic and smoke-filled battleground, Bellini's true prowess as a leader and fighter shone through. With an assault rifle firmly gripped in his hands, he moved with a calculated grace, his eyes scanning the area for any threats. The training he had undergone over the years now paid off as he expertly maneuvered through the mayhem.

As his finger tightened around the trigger, the air erupted with the thunderous sound of gunfire. Bellini's shots were precise and deadly, each bullet finding its mark with uncanny accuracy. His movements were fluid, almost dance-like, as he swiftly eliminated anyone foolish enough to cross his path.

With each pull of the trigger, Bellini displayed his class and the depth of his skill. He seamlessly transitioned from target to target, a force to be reckoned with in the heat of battle. His presence alone radiated power and authority, instilling fear in those who dared to stand against him.

As the smoke began to dissipate, the true extent of the chaos became apparent. Nadya, known for her lethal accuracy and fearless determination, emerged from the haze, her eyes focused and deadly. With calculated precision, she swiftly eliminated three army personnel who posed a threat to Bellini and the mission.

Though Nadya's actions were necessary to ensure their survival, a heavy weight settled upon her heart. The weight of the lives she had taken weighed heavily on her conscience.

She knew the cost of protecting her loved ones, but the guilt gnawed at her soul.

Finally, the Bellini family regrouped in their safe haven, their faces etched with a mixture of relief, exhaustion, and triumph. Lodovico, Bellini, Kerrim, and Mele sat together, their minds reeling from the intensity of the operation. Lodovico's voice filled the room as he spoke passionately, his anger and disappointment directed at Kerrim.

The room fell silent as Bellini, the calm and composed leader, interjected. His voice was firm yet soothing, his words carrying the weight of wisdom gained through years of experience. He acknowledged Kerrim's invaluable contributions, emphasizing the importance of unity within the family.

Bellini's words resonated deeply within Lodovico, slowly easing his anger and softening his stance. He began to recognize Kerrim's dedication and unwavering loyalty. The realization of the family's collective efforts began to wash away the remnants of his initial disappointment.

As the discussion continued late into the night, each member of the family shared their reflections on the mission. They marvelled at the resilience and resourcefulness that had carried them through the tumultuous ordeal. They understood that their strength lay not only in their individual talents but in their ability to come together as a cohesive unit.

The triumph of the mission served as a powerful reminder that the Bellini family was a force to be reckoned with. Despite the challenges and disagreements that had arisen along the way, their shared determination and unwavering bond had prevailed.

Meanwhile, outside the immediate vicinity of the firefight, a different kind of storm was brewing. The police and government agencies had been alerted to the Bellini family's daring rescue mission, and their focus was now directed towards apprehending those responsible. The news of Nadya's involvement, specifically her fatal encounter with three high-ranking army personnel, spread like wildfire.

The search intensified, with law enforcement agencies mobilizing their resources to capture Bellini and his family. The government officials were determined to bring an end to the Bellini empire, viewing it as a threat to the peace and stability they sought to uphold. Nadya, in particular, became a prime target due to her direct involvement in the fatal encounter.

As the investigation unfolded, the police combed through every shred of evidence, leaving no stone unturned. They delved into the family's connections, scrutinized their financial transactions, and gathered intelligence from informants on the ground. The net was closing in, and the pressure on the Bellini family grew exponentially.

Nadya, burdened with the weight of the lives she had taken, found herself at the centre of the storm. She knew that her actions had drawn the attention of the authorities, and the guilt gnawed at her conscience. The thought of being hunted haunted her every waking moment, as she grappled with the consequences of her choices.

In the face of the mounting search efforts, the Bellini family understood the gravity of the situation. They were well aware that their every move was being monitored, their every step scrutinized. They knew they had to tread carefully and adapt their strategies to outsmart their pursuers.

"Nadya," Bellini began, his voice laced with both love and concern, "we are facing an unprecedented threat from the government. They have the resources and the determination to bring us down. I cannot bear to see you in harm's way any longer. We must take precautions to ensure your safety."

Nadya nodded, understanding the gravity of the situation. She knew that her presence had become a liability, and the best course of action was to distance herself from the city where the government's reach was strongest. Her eyes met Bellini's, filled with a mix of sadness and determination.

"I understand, Bellini," she replied, her voice steady. "I will do whatever it takes to protect our family and our future. I am ready to go into hiding, to stay in the outskirts, away from the prying eyes of the government."

Bellini's expression softened, his hand reaching out to gently caress her cheek. "You are the strongest person I know, Nadya. I have complete faith in your ability to adapt and overcome. We will not let them break us."

With a heavy heart, Bellini made the necessary arrangements. He assigned four highly trained agents to accompany Nadya, individuals he trusted implicitly. These agents were seasoned professionals, skilled in evading detection and handling high-pressure situations. Their mission was clear: protect Nadya at all costs and ensure her safety during this perilous time.

The group retreated to a secluded hideout in the outskirts, a place where they could remain under the radar and maintain a low profile. They knew they had to be meticulous in their actions, leaving no traces or clues that could lead the government forces to their location.

Days turned into weeks as Nadya and her companions navigated the delicate balance of staying hidden while keeping a watchful eye on the unfolding events. They lived in constant vigilance, always on guard for any sign of impending danger. Their training kicked in; their instincts honed by years of experience in the treacherous world they inhabited.

During this period of seclusion, Nadya had time to reflect on her actions and the consequences they had brought upon the family. She grappled with guilt, haunted by the lives she had taken and the impact it had on her soul. But she also drew strength from her love for Bellini and the unwavering loyalty of the agents by her side.

The government's search grew more relentless with each passing day, their efforts fuelled by a sense of urgency to bring down the Bellini empire. But Nadya and her protectors remained hidden, their presence undetected as they patiently waited for the storm to subside.

As the weeks went by, hope and determination burned brightly within their hearts. They knew that their strength as a family and their unwavering resolve would carry them through this trial. Together, they would emerge stronger, ready to face whatever challenges lay ahead.
To be continued...

Turn Around

The scorching desert sun beat down mercilessly on the barren landscape, mirroring the desolation that filled Nadya's heart. Sitting alone amidst the vast expanse of sand, she was consumed by memories of Bellini and the life they once shared. The weight of loneliness pressed upon her, a heavy burden that seemed to grow with each passing moment.

In the distance, a cloud of dust stirred, drawing Nadya's attention. Her heart skipped a beat as she realized that a convoy of army officers was approaching. Panic and dread washed over her, knowing that this unexpected arrival could only mean one thing - her capture.

With a mix of resignation and defiance, Nadya rose to her feet, her gaze fixed on the approaching vehicles. The sound of engines grew louder, echoing through the barren landscape. As the convoy screeched to a halt before her, armed soldiers stepped out, their cold gazes penetrating her soul.

Nadya: "What do you want from me? Why have you come to take me?"

Officer: "You are under arrest. Surrender peacefully, and no harm will come to you."

Nadya's mind raced, searching for any means of escape. But she knew that resistance would be futile against the army's might. Reluctantly, she complied, allowing the officers to place her in restraints.

The journey to the air-tight prison was suffocating, both physically and emotionally. Nadya was confined to a small, dimly lit cell, her every movement restricted. The walls seemed to close in on her, as if mocking her futile attempts at freedom.

Days turned into nights; the passing of time marked only by the monotony of silence. Nadya's spirit remained unyielding, her determination to survive unbroken. She refused to succumb to the darkness that threatened to consume her.

News of Nadya's capture reached Bellini, igniting a firestorm of fury within him.

 The loss of his beloved companion, trapped behind those cold prison walls, was an unbearable agony. He knew that drastic measures were needed to bring her back to safety.
In a fit of rage, Bellini summoned the four agents responsible for Nadya's protection. The air in the room grew tense, charged with an undercurrent of impending doom.

Bellini: "You were entrusted with her safety, with protecting the very essence of our family. And yet, you allowed her to be taken away like a lamb to the slaughter."

Agent 1: "Boss, we never anticipated such a betrayal. We deeply regret our failure."

Bellini's eyes blazed with a mixture of grief and wrath; his voice laced with a hardened resolve.
Bellini: "Regret will not bring her back. Your incompetence has cost us dearly."

In one swift motion, Bellini drew his pistol, his hand steady and unwavering. Shots rang out, punctuating the room with a chilling finality. The agents fell to the ground, their bodies lifeless, a stark reminder of the consequences of failure.

As the echoes of the gunshots faded, Bellini's anger transformed into a steely determination. He knew that time was of the essence, that he had to find a way to rescue Nadya
from the clutches of her captors. The government had imprisoned her in an impenetrable fortress, cutting off all communication with the outside world. But Bellini's resolve burned brighter than ever, fuelled by love and an unbreakable bond.

With a resolute gaze, Bellini vowed to defy the odds, to orchestrate a plan that would bring Nadya back to his side, no matter the cost. The world may have imprisoned her physically, but her spirit remained unyielding, and Bellini would stop at nothing to set her free.

Nadya sat huddled in a corner of her dimly lit cell, tears streaming down her face as memories of her time with Bellini flooded her thoughts.

In the depths of her despair, she longed for his comforting presence, his strong arms embracing her, and his voice soothing her troubled soul.

As she reminisced, the echoes of their conversations resonated in her mind, as vivid as if he were standing right beside her.

Nadya: (whispering softly) "Bellini, my love, do you remember when we used to sit under the starlit sky, dreaming of a future filled with hope and freedom?"
In her mind's eye, she could see Bellini's charismatic smile and his unwavering gaze, filled with a mixture of love and determination.

Bellini: "Nadya, my heart, we have faced countless obstacles together, and we have always overcome them. We are bound by a love that transcends any prison walls. We will find a way to be together again."

Nadya clutched her heart, feeling the weight of their separation. The memories were bittersweet, fuelling her determination to endure and survive.

Nadya: (voice quivering) "Bellini, I can still hear your voice, urging me to stay strong, to never lose faith. But in this darkness, it's hard to find the light. I miss you, and I fear that I may never see your face again."

She closed her eyes, trying to conjure his image, his warmth, and the strength he always exuded.

Bellini: "Nadya, my love, you are the fire that burns within me. Your strength and resilience inspire me every day. Even in this darkness, remember that our love is a beacon of hope. We will find a way back to each other, no matter the obstacles that lie before us."

Nadya clung to his words, finding solace in the unwavering belief he held in their love. It fuelled her determination to survive, to endure the torment of her captivity.

Nadya: (whispering through tears) "I will hold onto your love, Bellini. It will be my guiding light, my source of strength. Together, we will overcome this ordeal, and I will be in your arms once again."

As the tears continued to fall, Nadya drew strength from the memories of their love, the promises they made to each other. In the depths of her despair, she found a flicker of hope, a resolve to withstand the trials ahead.

Nadya: (whispering into the void) "Bellini, I will survive for us, for our love. Until the day we are reunited, I will keep the flame burning, no matter the darkness that surrounds me."
With her heart filled with determination, Nadya vowed to endure the torment of her imprisonment, knowing that

their love would transcend the confines of her cell. And she held onto the belief that one day, their paths would intertwine again, and they would find solace in each other's arms.

The Very next day,

Affonso's heart raced as he received the call on the wired communication line. The voice on the other end greeted him, but its tone carried an underlying heaviness. It was a government official, and the news they had to deliver would shatter Affonso's world.

"I am from the government," the voice began, its words striking deep within Affonso's soul. "I regret to inform you that your girlfriend, Nadya, has been captured in connection with various cases and allegations."

Time seemed to stand still for Affonso as the weight of those words settled upon him. His mind raced, his heart ached, and a wave of anguish washed over him. He struggled to comprehend the devastating news he had just received.

"Wha-what do you mean?" Affonso stammered, his voice trembling with a mix of fear and sorrow. "Captured? What happened?"

The government official's voice remained stoic, lacking any trace of empathy. "I regret to inform you that she has been killed," the voice revealed, the words hanging in the air like a dark cloud. "The circumstances surrounding her death cannot be disclosed at this time."

Affonso's world shattered into a million pieces. The room around him blurred as tears welled up in his eyes. The pain of loss engulfed him, leaving him breathless and empty. Nadya, his love, his partner, his everything, was gone. The weight of grief settled heavily upon his shoulders, threatening to crush him under its unbearable burden.

Anger erupted within Affonso, fuelling a fire deep within his soul. In a voice filled with determination, he declared, "This government, these individuals who took her from me, they will pay. They will face the consequences of their actions. I swear upon her memory that I will do whatever it takes to bring them down, to seek justice for Nadya."

With every ounce of strength he possessed, Affonso vowed to rise against the government that had stolen his love away. The pain transformed into a burning determination, propelling him forward on a path of revenge and justice. He knew the road ahead would be treacherous, but he would not rest until he had dismantled those responsible for Nadya's untimely demise.

In the depths of his sorrow, Affonso found a newfound resolve, a flicker of defiance that would fuel his every action. The loss of Nadya had ignited a fire within him, one that would guide him on a perilous journey to seek retribution.

The government had unwittingly awakened a force they could not control, and they would soon learn the price of their actions.

As the call ended, Affonso was left alone with his grief and his unwavering determination. He would not let Nadya's death be in vain.
 With each step forward, he would carry her memory, seeking justice and a reckoning that would shake the foundations of the very government that had taken her life.

And so, in the depths of his sorrow, Affonso vowed to honour Nadya's memory and bring an end to the tyranny that had shattered their world. The battle lines had been drawn, and the stage was set for a clash of epic proportions.

 The government had underestimated the resolve of a grieving man, and they would soon face the consequences of their actions.

Chapter 9 came to a close, leaving behind a trail of grief, anger, and a relentless pursuit of justice. Affonso would not rest until he had avenged Nadya's untimely demise and brought about the downfall of those who had torn them apart. The stage was set for an epic showdown, and the world would soon bear witness to the fury of a man pushed to his limits.

Done And Dusted

As the plans for their assault on the government neared completion, Affonso was approached by Kerrim with a revelation that would shatter his anger-fuelled resolve. Kerrim's voice carried a mixture of relief and caution as he spoke.

"Affonso, there's something you need to know," Kerrim began, his eyes filled with a mix of concern and reassurance. "The government's claim about Nadya's capture and death was a fabrication, a ploy to manipulate your emotions and incite you to act impulsively."

Affonso's heart skipped a beat as the weight of Kerrim's words sank in. A torrent of emotions surged through him, a mixture of relief and confusion. Nadya was alive? The thought both elated him and left him questioning the motives behind the government's deception.

"She's safe, Affonso," Kerrim continued, his voice steady. "She's being held in custody, awaiting trial. We have a plan to ensure her escape during the court proceedings. But we must tread carefully, for the government will be watching our every move."

A sense of calm washed over Affonso, alleviating the anger that had consumed him. He took a deep breath, allowing the truth to sink in. The weight of vengeance was replaced by the reassurance that Nadya was alive and, albeit captive, still within their reach.

With a renewed sense of purpose, Affonso turned his attention to the immediate task at hand. He gathered Lodovico, Antonino, Heinz, and Kerrim, the core members of their family, to organize an event—a celebration of their recent successes and a show of solidarity for Nadya's security.

The venue was transformed into a magnificent space, adorned with elegant decorations and soft, warm lighting. Affonso, dressed in a tailored black suit, exuded an air of confidence, yet his eyes betrayed a subtle hint of concern. He couldn't shake the feeling that something was amiss, a sense of foreboding that lingered in the depths of his being.

As the guests began to arrive, their attire reflecting a blend of sophistication and resilience, Affonso welcomed each one with a genuine smile. But beneath his calm demeanour, his senses were heightened, attuned to every subtle shift in the atmosphere. He had become a master of reading the room, a skill honed through years of navigating the treacherous world they inhabited.

The night was filled with laughter, music, and spirited conversations, the ambiance masking the underlying tension that coursed through their veins. Affonso kept a watchful eye on his family, their expressions a tapestry of determination and hope. Their unity was palpable, a silent agreement to stand together against the forces that sought to tear them apart.

As the evening progressed, Affonso found himself in deep conversation with Lodovico. Their exchange was a mixture of reminiscing about their shared history and discussing the challenges that lay ahead. Affonso's voice resonated with a blend of optimism and caution as he reassured Lodovico of their ability to navigate the turbulent waters ahead.

"We've come so far, my friend," Affonso said, his voice laced with emotion. "And though the road ahead may be treacherous, we will face it together. Nadya's safety and our family's well-being are our top priorities. We must remain steadfast in our resolve, yet ever vigilant of the threats that surround us."

Lodovico nodded, his eyes reflecting a combination of gratitude and determination. "You've always been the voice of reason, Affonso. I trust your judgment, and I stand by your side, ready to face whatever comes our way."

As the night drew to a close, and the guests bid their farewells, Affonso felt a sense of quiet satisfaction. They had forged ahead, armed with knowledge and a plan, ready to free Nadya from the clutches of an unjust system. The events of the past had only served to strengthen their resolve, fuelling their determination to dismantle the government's oppressive grip.

As the night drew to a close, Affonso and Kerrim found solace in each other's company. They sat in a dimly lit room, savouring a rare moment of respite amidst the chaos that surrounded them. Their glasses clinked, the sound echoing in the silence as they shared a drink.

Affonso's gaze wandered to the distance, his thoughts drifting back to his early days, when life was a constant struggle and survival meant navigating treacherous paths. He spoke, his voice tinged with both nostalgia and pain.

"You know, Kerrim, my father always told me that strength comes from enduring the toughest of circumstances. He wanted me to break free from the chains that bound our family, to rise above our past and create a new legacy."

Kerrim listened intently, his own memories intermingling with Affonso's words. He thought of the servant who had raised him, instilling in him values and principles that shaped the man he had become. He responded, his voice laced with a mix of gratitude and uncertainty.

"Affonso, my father figure, the one who raised me, was a servant in our household. He was the epitome of strength and resilience. He always said that blood didn't define family, but rather the bonds we forge."

Affonso's brow furrowed; his curiosity piqued. He couldn't help but ask the question that had haunted Kerrim for years. "Kerrim, after all this time, don't you wonder who your real father was?"

Kerrim met Affonso's gaze, his expression a mixture of contemplation and resignation. "I've pondered that question countless times, my friend. But perhaps some secrets are better left buried. The man who raised me, who taught me to be honourable and just, that's the only father I'll ever need."

Their conversation hung in the air, a reflection of the complexities of their lives. But their moment of contemplation was interrupted by the shrill ring of the wired communication system. Affonso's hand instinctively reached for the receiver, a mix of apprehension and hope coursing through him.

"Nadya?" Affonso's voice trembled with anticipation as he spoke her name.

On the other end of the line, Nadya's voice cracked with fear and anguish. "Affonso, I've been sentenced to death. They're going to execute me. Why didn't you come for me? Why didn't you save me?"

Confusion gripped Affonso's heart, his emotions colliding within him like a storm. "Nadya, what are you talking about? We're coming for you. We'll do whatever it takes to save you."
But Nadya's words pierced through his shattered heart. "There was someone, Affonso. A man named Marco Bellini. He claimed to be your father. He said... he said you abandoned me."

Affonso's world crumbled around him. The room seemed to spin as he tried to make sense of the revelation. Marco Bellini? There was no other Bellini they knew. The weight of uncertainty settled upon him, and he knew that the truth he sought lay hidden in the shadows.

The conversation hung in a fragile pause, leaving Affonso with more questions than answers. The revelation had shaken his foundation, stirring up a storm of emotions. The bond between him and Nadya was strong, but the Specter of doubt now loomed overhead, threatening to unravel everything they held dear.

As Affonso turns around, Kerrim steps forward, a malevolent grin playing on his lips. The room is cloaked in an eerie silence, the air thick with tension. Their eyes lock, and Affonso senses an overwhelming darkness emanating.

Kerrim comes from darkness and stabs Affonso with a sharp knife, his pistol on Affonso's throat, then struck the knife in his stomach, and then with a voice filled with venom, Kerrim reveals the shocking truth. "Affonso, it's time for you to know who I really am," he sneers. "I am Macro Bellini, your brother. Our father, Lucas, was not only your father but mine as well."

Affonso's breath catches in his throat, his mind reeling with the weight of this revelation. The pieces of his fractured past suddenly fit together, forming a devastating picture of betrayal and abandonment.

The room seems to close in around him as he struggles to comprehend the magnitude of Kerrim's words.

Kerrim's voice drips with bitterness as he continues, relishing in his moment of triumph. "Our father left us behind, casting us aside while he built his empire. But I never forgot, Affonso. The pain, the loneliness—it fuelled a thirst for vengeance within me. And now, the time has come for you to pay for his sins."

A mix of emotions floods Affonso's being—anger, confusion, and a profound sense of loss. The brother he never knew existed stands before him, a Specter of retribution. His fists clench, his heart torn between the love he still carries for his father and the desire for justice.

Macro/Kerrim with shrilled and painful voice says ' You know, how tough was it for me to even survive? you were enjoying a three-time meal in your big house and I was out there surviving for a single time food"

Kerrim's eyes burn with a mixture of hatred and envy as he looks upon Affonso, his voice dripping with venomous contempt. "You have no idea, Affonso, the life that could have been mine. The riches, the power, the respect. Everything you took for granted, I longed for with every fibre of my being."

He paces back and forth, his words punctuated by his fists clenched in frustration. "While you reveled in luxury, basking in the spoils of our father's success, I endured years of struggle and pain. I clawed my way up from the dirt, fighting tooth and nail for a mere scrap of what was rightfully mine."

With a mix of anger and sadness, Kerrim reaches into his pocket and pulls out an old, worn-out photograph. He slowly unfolds it and presents it to Affonso.
In the photograph, Affonso sees his father, Lucas, standing beside a woman he recognizes as his mother. There's a sense of familiarity in the way they hold each other, their smiles revealing a shared bond. Affonso's heart skips a beat as he realizes the truth that Kerrim has been hiding all along.

Kerrim's voice trembles with emotion as he speaks, "This is my mother and that man beside her is our father, Lucas. Look closely, Affonso. Look at their faces, the way they embrace. They were once a family before everything fell apart."

Affonso's eyes well up with tears as the realization sinks in. He looks from the photograph to Kerrim, searching for the resemblance, and finds it in their eyes, their shared features, and the pain etched on both their faces.

"You and I, we share the same blood," Kerrim continues, his voice now softer, filled with longing. "I was abandoned, left to fend for myself. But in pursuit of different paths, I found you once again, though circumstances have driven us apart."

The weight of their shared history hangs heavy in the air, and Affonso's anger begins to subside, replaced by a mix of sorrow, regret, and a newfound sense of connection. The revelations have shaken him to his core, forcing him to confront the consequences of his father's actions.

His voice rises, echoing through the room, as he continues his tirade. "I watched as you were handed opportunities on a silver platter, connections, and Favors bestowed upon you without question. Meanwhile, I forged my own path, surrounded by treachery and betrayal at every turn."

Kerrim's eyes bore into Affonso's, his voice a venomous whisper. "Do you know what it feels like, Affonso? To see the world shower, you with adoration and privilege, while I stood on the sidelines, invisible and forgotten? I was the one who should have been living that heaven life, revelling in the spoils of our father's empire."

He takes a step closer, his voice now a chilling whisper that carries a sense of quiet menace. "But now, it ends. Your reign, your illusion of superiority—it crumbles before me. No longer will I be the forgotten brother, the one overshadowed by your shadow, it is my time to rise, to claim what should have been rightfully mine."

"You think this is justice?" Affonso's voice trembles with a mixture of anguish and defiance. "Taking revenge on me won't right the wrongs of our past. It only perpetuates the cycle of pain and destruction."

Kerrim's eyes narrow, the fires of hatred burning brightly within them. He raises a pistol, pressing it against Affonso's temple, relishing in the power he holds over his brother's life.

 "It ends here, Affonso," he hisses. "Your life ends here, just as our father's legacy did."

" My brother, bonds and families are never meant by blood but by loyalty, in the end, now you've become a lifeless body, and the life was taken by your own brother by blood, how is that feeling, Affonso?"

"Right now, I feel that I have whispered vengeance in your soul, Bye-Bye my friend, Goodnight…….Forever."